Augustus Hoppin

Recollections of Auton House

A Book for Children

Augustus Hoppin

Recollections of Auton House
A Book for Children

ISBN/EAN: 9783337215699

Printed in Europe, USA, Canada, Australia, Japan

Cover: Foto ©Andreas Hilbeck / pixelio.de

More available books at **www.hansebooks.com**

AUTON HOUSE.

"*Olim meminisse juvabit.*"

RECOLLECTIONS OF AUTON HOUSE.

A Book for Children.

WITH ILLUSTRATIONS.

By C. AUTON.

BOSTON:
HOUGHTON, MIFFLIN AND COMPANY.
The Riverside Press, Cambridge.
1881.

The Riverside Press, Cambridge:
Electrotyped and Printed by H. O. Houghton & Co.

PREFACE.

THESE reminiscences are written to satisfy the Auton who composed them, and to amuse the Autons who may read them. Grown-up people never cease to be young. They are only old boys with hats and whiskers, and old girls with frizettes and eye-glasses, that's all. There are many Auton houses in the land, and lots of Auton children wandering over it, but the original Auton House is gone forever, and we can only catch the echo of its revelry in our ear, and detect a smack of its good cheer lingering on our tongue.

As an old-fashioned dish, now and then, is not unpalatable, so perhaps a few chapters of reminiscences may be tolerated, provided they do not overtax our patience by their platitudes.

CONTENTS.

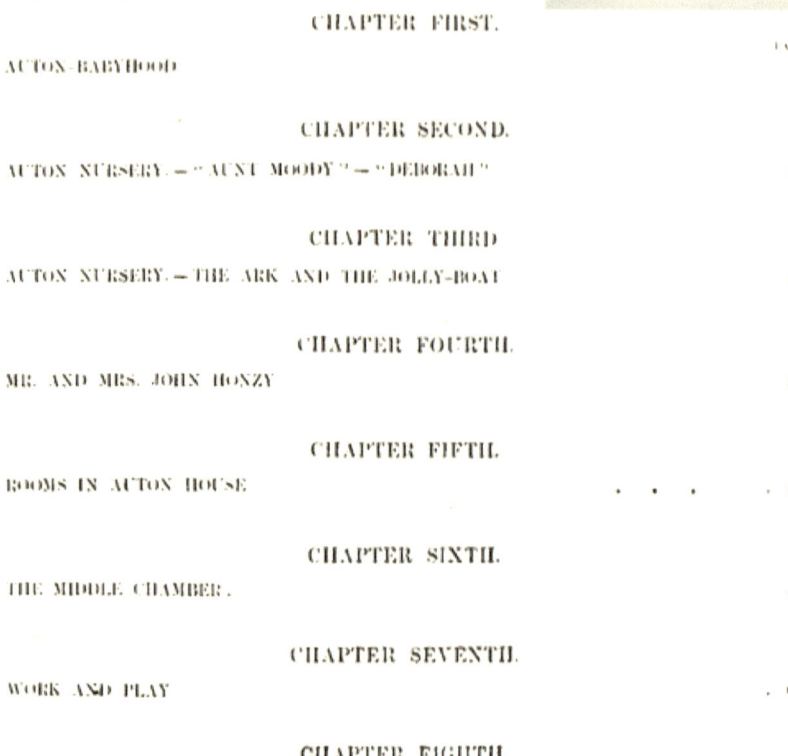

viii

CONTENTS.

CHAPTER NINTH.

PAGE

CHAPTER TENTH.

CHAPTER ELEVENTH.

CHAPTER TWELFTH.

RECOLLECTIONS OF AUTON HOUSE.

CHAPTER FIRST.

AUTON - BABYHOOD.

Y name is C. Auton, a boy-baby. They blew in my face to keep me alive. My parents had so many children that my advent troubled nobody but my mother and Doctor Posset.

I struggled with existence in the usual senseless manner. The first liquid I ever swallowed was a spoonful of tepid sugar-and-water.

I lay on Miss Betsey Arnold's lap for hours, so poor and weak as hardly to be able to keep together. The whole lookout of life was sad and unnatural. I had no idea I should be such a fool, and was ashamed to be unable to hold up my head. I found, also, to my chagrin, that Miss Betsey's supporting hand behind my ears was necessary to keep me from tumbling together into a little heap. My eyes got constantly crossed looking at Miss Betsey's gold spectacles, and I was continually trying to see how wide I could stretch my mouth, and what new grimaces I could make at invisible people.

When I did this in my sleep Miss Betsey said it was the wind in my
stomach. My poor little knees were dreadfully red and mottled,
and when I lay on my back they came way up over my head.

I made frequent attempts to stick my finger through that soft
spot between the sutures on the top of my cranium. People who
saw my little finger-nail pronounced it the smallest on record.
When Miss Betsey and I were alone I inspected my digits to dis-
cover what there was so "awful cunning" about them. When the
parson came to see me nurse asked him if I was not a "beauty."
The conscientious man, I am told, got over the difficulty by saying,
"Well, he *is* a baby." When I was sufficiently cohesive to bear pin-
ning, I passed my time driveling over Miss Betsey's finger, and
repeating the inane expression "a-goo!"

Grown folks know little about the real trouble of "being dressed."
Prinking for balls and dressing for dinners is nothing to the ma-
tutinal lavations of babyhood. It is the bore of infancy. Miss
Betsey was a "cleaner" in every sense of the word; and when
she once "put her hand to the plow" she went straight through,
regardless of screams, and kicking the air, and loss of breath.

, Almost the first thing Miss Betsey did to me, after supporting
my neck in the bath-tub to prevent my head from bobbing under
the water, was to let me drip on the blanket. Then she rubbed my
back into a bright ruby-color, and "adjusted" the apology for a
shirt over that hunchy strip of wrinkled flannel which pinched my
sides underneath. This ruffled "apology" was three or four times
too wide for its length. Miss Betsey first folded it in a broad
plait in front, while I lay on my back; then, after I had been
flopped over on my face across her knees, like a batch of dough, she
took another broad plait in the rear. To keep this skimpy thing in

place, came the snug-fitting, long-skirted flannel petticoat sewed on
to a cotton waist, and pinned pretty tight. Miss Betsey always
meant her "things" to stay. After this — like an extinguisher —
over the head came the gossamer linen slip with its frills and its
insertions, its armlets and its shield-pins, — the three-cornered bib
with its shield-pin, — the enormous scarf with its shield-pin, and the
puff and the powder, and the hair parted at the side with a curl in
the shape of a rolling-billow on the top of the head. I was then
what was called "dressed." But all these different layers of clothing pinched and squeezed me so that I screamed with discomfort.
Miss Betsey said "C. Auton was hungry," — so I was instantly laid
on my back again and filled up with milk and water. She dexter-
ously caught the overflowing streams in the pap-spoon, as they
meandered down the corners of my mouth, and scooped them cleverly back again into their proper channel, saying all the time,
"There! there!" Then I was jounced and trotted at a pleasant
family gait, until my little crowded, wheezing, and rolling stomach
had wrestled with and overcome the lacteal ocean poured into it —
when Miss Betsey "eased up," and my internal revolutions ceased.

The deep mahogany cradle in which all
the Auton-babies passed their younger
days stands out like a telegraph pole
along the path of my earliest memory.
Oh, that wonderful cradle! Oh, that deep,
respectable cradle! Oh, that rich, mahogany cradle! Its color, acquired by age,
and the constant rubbing of little boys'
trousers, resembled that of the wonderful
gingerbread which "Old Rosannah, the

cook," used to bake for us, and nothing could be richer than that.
The hood of that rocking hammock had a graceful slant. The
brass handles at either end were bright as bright could be. The
roof was fastened with brass-headed nails, and the rockers had just
the right bevel to invite slumber. One of the roof-boards was
cracked, and the light played through the aperture — first darkness, then light, then darkness, then light — as our baby-heads
went wagging to and fro while Miss Betsey did the rocking.

Talk about the sweet slumber which follows honest toil! It is
nothing to the peaceful naps in that old cradle. I can see it now
with its clean draperies wooing us to its soft embrace.

Before Miss Betsey laid us in it she leaned forward to " make it
up," while the baby hung dangling and dozing over her left arm
the while. First came the long bolster-pillow in the body of the
cradle. Then the shorter one at the top, with a little soft valley in
it for the head to lie in. Then came the baby — so sleepy ! — so
limp with nodding ! He was laid gently on his right side, with his
thumb in his mouth and a small milk-blister on his upper lip. The
left arm — that one which had been vaccinated, and which was
beginning to " take " — softly placed outside the blanket. " Sh !
Sh ! Sh ! There ! there !" The rocking stopped. C. Auton was
asleep.

Miss Betsey Arnold was the queen of nurses. I shall never forget her kindness during that perilous epoch of evolution. I shall
ever thank her for winking at my sucking the wash-rag during my
morning bath, and while she was rummaging my basket for the next
layer of clothes. It was a sweet privilege — now so tardily acknowledged. Dear Miss Betsey ! In a better land than this you
will reap your own nursing reward. That " innumerable caravan "

which you so gracefully welcomed on this side of life will greet you there on the other with loud acclaim.

Big and little voices will call you " Auntie."

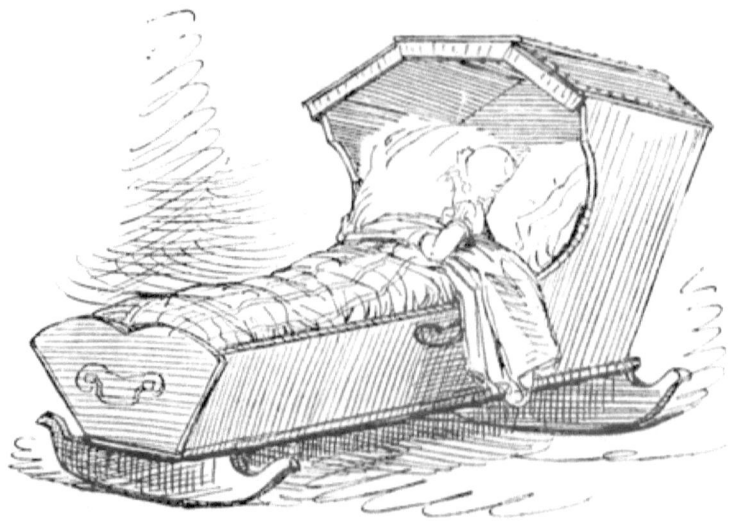

My mother had twelve Auton-babies. One failed to attain maturity, and that left eleven. They arrived in the following order:—

J. AUTON,
    A. AUTON (girl),
        T. AUTON,
            S. AUTON (girl),
                F. AUTON,
                    H. AUTON,
                        E. AUTON (girl),
                            W. AUTON,
                                A. AUTON,
                                    H. AUTON (girl),
                                        C. AUTON.

None of these Autons were prodigies, although several of them were "unkimmon clever" and "bright as buttons."

They were bred in a famous nursery, under the surveillance of several quite remarkable women; two of whom were named "Aunt Moody" and "Deborah." In this wonderful spot they passed their happy adolescence, until they were ready to cut loose from apron-strings and do battle in the great world themselves.

For the amusement of other Autons throughout Christendom, I will in the following chapters give a description of these two Auton nurses, and some account of the marvelous transactions which were performed in that celebrated mansion for the space of a generation — during which time different sets of Autons were graduating from and entering into this blessed goal of their tenderer years.

CHAPTER SECOND.

AUTON NURSERY.

"AUNT MOODY" — "DEBORAH."

PRICELESS boon in the nursery — next to a good mother — is a faithful nurse. I don't mean that modern female nondescript with a Normandy cap and a mouth full of foreign language, but a kind-hearted Puritan, of good judgment and common sense ; one who remembered General Washington, and who lived for the children under her care rather than for so much a month. Unhappily this species is nearly extinct — buried beneath the new kinks of modern nurseryism. Still, however, a traveler here and there totters across our pathway, reminding us of her long life of self-sacrifice and devotion.

"Aunt Moody" and "Deborah" were two old-fashioned, long-suffering, sweet-tempered children-lovers. To us they seemed to have been born in that nursery, or, for aught we knew, were coexistent with the Flood. Whenever they "went out" it was as much of a circumstance to the whole household as one of Mother Auton's evening parties, or a Thanksgiving dinner. Whenever they "dressed up" the children immediately stopped play, gathered about their knees, and plied them with the most impertinent questions — handled

and fingered their old finery with a license which the extraordinary
circumstances of the occasion alone warranted. "Aunt Moody" and
"Deborah" were as much of an institution in the Auton nursery as
the old four-poster bedstead: or the nursery closet where the medicines were kept; or the top cupboard where the "balm" and the
"catnip" and the "elder" sent out their perfume; or the rug by

the nursery fire where the boys
got to sleep on Saturday nights,
waiting to be washed; or the trundle-bed under the big bed, where
we were all stowed away in peace,
— or any other of those household penates connected with our
earthly paradise. I can only speak
of "Aunt Moody" with a meas-
ured amount of assurance, as she
was associated with that former
régime. when the first stratum of
Autons held the nursery under
their domination. The reign of
"Deborah" (which marked the epoch of the incursion of the
younger branch into the nursery which took possession. like the
ancient Huns. of what. to us. constituted the whole known world)
is the occasion affording me opportunity to speak with confidence
and certainty.

"Aunt Moody" was a little, clean, old woman with a very large
nose and a ruffled mob-cap not unlike "Old Mother Hubbard's."
This cap had no strings, but was kept in place by a wide black rib-
bon with an Alsacian bow at the top of it. Originally she had had

large quantities of double-chin, but this feature, through lapse of years and cares of the nursery, had dwindled both in comeliness and substance, so that it now served only as the plaything of the younger children, who fondled it with tender emotion. To us youngsters there was something strange and uncanny about Aunt Moody, and we listened with bated breath to her stories of "Sister Carstoff" and "Brother Ben," the sea-captain; and this strangeness was only increased by the funniest-looking thumb which she had, and the queerest sort of a big toe which we used to catch sight of on Saturday nights, two facts which completed the romantic and peculiar impression of this old lady. But for all that she was a dear creature, self-sacrificing and long-suffering, and to her unwearying counsel and unremitting care the older Autons are indebted for a good deal of their "bringing-up."

Whenever the children took the census of the family Aunt Moody came next in order to us. She was followed by Rosannah, the black cook, and Freeborn (pronounced Fre'bun), the black waiter, and the old wooden pump in the kitchen, and "Sterling," the yellow-eyed cat, and the oval brick oven, where the Sunday-morning breakfast was baked, and the horseshoes hanging on the old crane, and the bright tin-kitchen before the wood fire, and the Johnny-cake board, and many other objects of affection in Auton House of so much individualism and character as to entitle them to a position as members of the family.

People said Aunt Moody had been married, and that there was a

2

son or daughter in Swansea, or Rehoboth, or some other (to us)
foreign city. But if so "Old Moody" never "turned up" to dis-
turb her, and she was left unmolested to complete her blameless,
self-sacrificing mission untrammeled by any uxorious responsibil-
ities.

Aunt Moody wore a frizette, and T. Auton on one occasion

pulled it off,
leaving her
aged poll de-
fenseless and
bare, but the
dear old body
immediately
forgave him,
and showed
this forgive-
ness by snatch-
ing the same
boy off the
"forestick"
where he had

sat down and caught fire — when, throwing him on the rug, she
"put him out" with a pitcher of hot water.

It would be a subject for a clever artist to depict, this faithful
creature amidst a bevy of pretty boys and girls, moving hither,
and yon, settling disputes, soothing ruffled feelings, chiding the uproarious, and chasing unruly offenders under the bed. Her surest
method of dislodging them from this hiding-place was a coal of fire
in the tongs, which she would thrust into their lair, repeating all
the while her favorite oath, "Burn yer boots! burn yer boots!"

When Aunt Moody left Auton House forever, the nursery was hung in sackcloth. Her loss seemed to us irreparable. No more queer-looking big toes Saturday nights! No more funny-looking thumbs to fondle! No more double-chins to caress! Our "dolls were stuffed with sawdust." The night of her departure was kept a secret from the younger children. The new nurse who was to fill the gap left by our ancient friend was instructed to comfort

the disconsolate ones when they woke up by taking their hands, as Aunt Moody used to do; but the ruse proved unavailing, for the moment they missed that friendly but stubbed thumb on the strange hand stretched out to them in the darkness they screamed out, "Aunt Moody's gone!" "Aunt Moody's gone!" "Who is this old thing in bed with us?" "We won't have you!" "We hate you!" And away went the blankets and the sheets, and out jumped a brood of young Autons, with heads like mops, in night-gowns and night-drawers, howling like a pack of savages. That was a night to be remembered.

"DEBORAH."

EBORAH, or, as we called her, "Deb-'rah," was a little brunette woman, weighing about one hundred and twelve pounds, but every one of those pounds was a good one. Her whole life was a vicarious one. She no more thought of neglecting her daily duty than she did of omitting to wash our faces; and this was sometimes rather a delicate operation, because our little noses would become chapped and inflamed by the cold, and our grimy hands at night were, what she used to call. "A sight to behold," the grime being lackered on. Deborah's career was one prolonged exhibition of self-sacrifice. See how much she did for us, and how very little for herself!

For our sakes she kept in that nursery from morning till night for over a generation.

She sat up till midnight ironing our collars and plaiting our ruffles, while her parboiled thumbs were bleeding from the cracks which cold and constant washing had produced. She never had a good square night's rest for thirty years.

For our sakes she had the worst form of dyspepsia — eating her meals so irregularly, and at unheard-of hours. If necessary, she swept up after us twenty times a day without a whimper. She slept on the edge of the bed until she became a callous old woman. She warded off many a maternal castigation, and meekly allowed all of us to "pile on" her back, to sop her scanty front hair with water, twist it into curls and frizzles and "comb it to death," while she, poor soul! was nodding from sheer exhaustion, and enduring these indignities without a murmur. And what did she do for herself? She may have laid up her wages, but we didn't know anything about that. She was content with one dull-colored gown, and one apron for week days, and a Sunday one for other occasions.

If she ever had a lover we children must have frightened him
away. She had a brother "Ellerey," who was a truckman, and a
sister-in-law with one little stiff arm, whom she called "Ruby," and
"Anna Maria," her niece, who was pretty, and had weak eyes, and
a pair of prunella shoes — and that was all. The rest of her life and
the rest of her thoughts were devoted to us. And in return for it
we provoked her, and plagued her, and combed her hair all out, and
almost worried her life out, until she was thin enough to blow away,
and weary enough to lie down and die. If there is but one saint
in heaven Deb'rah is that one. If love, and devotion, and duty
ever bring their own reward there is a halo of glory about our
Deb'rah's head which can never fade away. She came from Tiv-
erton, and her complexion was sallow.

It is singular how an old nurse like this is indissolubly connected
in the memory with every act of one's youthful life. Reminiscences
of both joy and sorrow ever bring back with them that faded image.
Whenever W. Auton and I had new suits of clothes come home from
"Aunt Nancy Miller's" (the nursery tailoress) smelling of snuff and
beeswax, Deb'rah was the girl who first buttoned them up for us.
When March, April, and May came round, the season to take the
"spring medicine," Deb'rah stood ready with the sulphur and mo-
lasses, to deal out to each child in procession that gritty sweetness, a
panacea for all ills. When a sudden attack of "stomach out of order"
made its hated appearance, and the lukewarm "salts," or the "debil-
itating" *steeped physic*, were set in the washbowl to cool, that same
long-suffering creature labored with us to "be good boys and take
it," and stood ready with the bit of orange to clap in our mouths the
instant the dose was swallowed, and took us to her attenuated bosom
to comfort us, until the taste was out of our mouths.

Oh! that dreadful castor oil and ipecacuanha period! "Shall I ever forget thee?" She brought forth the lukewarm draught. There it was smoking and cooling in the white washbowl. We stopped our play to sniff its odious contents. We turned up our noses at the bare suggestion. We swore that we would "never, no never, take the darned stuff," but she begged and implored and

prayed us to "just go and swallow it like little men." But not until we had struck her, and kicked her, and she had finally threatened to call in Mother Auton, with that "legendary medicine spoon" which either strangled the boy or lodged the dose safely in his stomach, did we break furiously away from her apron-strings, approach the villainous decoction, and, with faces resembling that of Mephistopheles, drain the vile cup to the "bitter end."

This subject of medicines naturally leads me into our great nursery-closet where all the different medicaments were kept. When I call to mind the contents of the three shelves on the right-hand side as you entered that closet, I wonder that there is a single Auton left alive, or, at least, unparalyzed, to tell the tale. The first sight revealed a sugar-bowl with no cover, which contained that "whited sepulchre" — epsom salts. The syrup-of-squills bottle, with its sugared nozzle, stood next to it. Then came "Old Reliable," the castor-oil tank. How hard that dose was to swallow! almost impossible to get *all* of it out from the table-spoon, yet every bit *had* to be scooped into the mouth with our upper lip before the orange came to take the taste out. Here stands the spirits of nitre for fever, and there the essence of peppermint for stomach-ache. Next to this comes the deadly paregoric for crying babies, then a little bottle labeled "Balsam of Life," then a dreadfully bad-tasting compound called "*Elixir Salutis*," next to this stands the essence of red lavender — jolly on sugar! Then, away back there, in a round glass bottle, stood the "Elixir Pro." — we used to call it "Lex'y Pro." This last medicine was "child's play" to that horrid "Piery," ah! so bitter! Deb'rah called it "Verm'fug," and it was a good one. And after this what we called "Epekak," and, oh my! how effective. Then came all sorts and kinds of pill boxes and salves and cough mixtures. One of these compositions in an earthen jar, called "Manton's Compound," was rather palatable. The licorice part was "So-so" to take, but its other ingredients made us sick. Then followed white papers of senna leaves and manna, with here and there a bit of stick-licorice and a small lump of manna. This latter substance we always believed to be the true manna eaten by the Israelites for forty years in their wanderings. Then came packages of boneset and thoroughwort. Then a bottle of apple-balsam for wounds. Then old pieces of flannel skirts and other things to dip into hot rum when folks were in pain. Then New England rum. Then a broken teacup containing "Burgundy pitch" to spread on plasters for the "smalls of backs," and the old case-knife to spread it on with lying beside the cup. Then

came lint and bees-wax, and balsam of Tolu, and dry magnesia in square bottles, for heart-burn, and ever so many more frightful nostrums. It is a cause for thanksgiving that we survived all these "lions in our path."

On the left side of this closet lay the sweet herbs brought to us every year by old Miss Burden and Nancy Speywood. There was the aromatic catnip, and the cooling balm, the sweet everlasting, and the bitter chamomile. I shall never forget the refreshment which Deb'rah's cold balm-tea, poured from a broken-nosed teapot, gave to our parched throats, after the Doctor had forbidden us to touch cold water, during fever attacks.

These fragrant bundles of nature's perfumery were piled, one above another, on the upper shelves of the old closet, in clean, white, cotton bags; and they served as agreeable foils to counteract the deadly characteristics of the opposite side.

Among all this scented herbage we passed many a fleeting hour.
W. Auton (boy), beautiful as the day, with chestnut curls and rosy,
pouting lips, would climb to the top shelf, flageolet in hand, and
buried there in this fragrant retreat would discourse long repeti-
tions of "Lord dismiss us" and "Auld lang Syne," in order to
drown the squeals of the younger children and the fat girls of
the family, who, acting out the play of "market," were making
believe being butchered for Christmas, and cut up into joints by
the older boys.

CHAPTER THIRD.

AUTON NURSERY.

THE ARK AND THE JOLLY-BOAT.

OAH'S ark and the jolly - boat, by which I mean the big four-poster and the trundle-bed underneath it, have sheltered more square yards of children within their wide, straddling sides than any other two private beds in New England.

To enter the ark we needed a chair, to board the jolly-boat we had only to tumble in. The trundle-bed was shoved under the big one during the day and drawn out at night. These beds held different sets of children at different epochs. Once the two afforded nightly domicile for no less than six boy and girl Autons. Besides these, Deb'rah, of course, was curled up somewhere on the edge of the bed, on a space scarcely wide enough to rest a teacup. In the morning the " baby," whoever it might be, was set in the midst of the charmèd circle, to which was often added the new kitten, a fresh puppy, or somebody's black boy. Bottled up within this company was a tremendous amount of latent fun and animal spirits, ready at any instant to break out and join the "dreadful revelry" about to begin. It is impossible to describe all the wonderful plays and journeys taken, — the babels and bedlams let loose — the hootings and shoutings and screams which proceeded, on such occasions, from the warm depths of these resting-places of my childhood. I will endeavor, however, to give an idea of several of the more prominent and fascinating fandangoes, as specimens of the rest.

I must premise this description by making a remark about the nursery night-dress of that period. All the girls wore nightcaps with ruffles on the edge. As to that matter Mother Auton and Deb'rah were all in the fashion; mother's cap was high behind, the ruffles coming all over her face and concealing every feature but her nose, while Deb'rah's " was smaller, and used to get askew" in the morning, after the whole family had clambered across her face to see who could be first at the fire to dress.

All the boy Autons wore night-drawers, tied behind with running strings, once at the neck, and then again at the waist. These garments always "gaped" a little in the back, but this only made it more fun to jump out of them after they had been tied, and then stick our legs quickly back again before Deb'rah saw us.

Every Auton child said his prayers.

First came the prayer beginning "Now another day is gone." In this petition there are lines like these: " See how my childhood runs to waste;" " My sins how great a sum!"

This passage puzzled us much, and we used to inspect each other very closely to see if we were actually "running to waist." We concluded, also, that as the prayer said that our sins were a "greater sum" they probably must be, although we failed to see the force of the expression. One of the children explained it by saying it had "something to do with salvation," and that settled it. After this came the prayer, "Now I lay me," etc.

To us, this was some sort of an animal, a Llama, which we resembled, lying down to sleep. Religion seemed queer to us then, and came hard. After our devotions we prepared ourselves for the night and generally consumed large quantities of cold, shortened, flour Johnny-cake, which made us very thirsty, and got the bed full of dried crumbs. These would roll under us and prick our warm rosy skins, so that Deb'rah had to come and scrape them up in the palm of her hand, while we squatted on the outside of the bed in our night-clothes. These operations, preliminary to sleep, ended by a "drink of water" all round, and Auton Nursery then became actually quiet.

H. Auton was an older boy than some of the others. He slept in the ark, and had his own way on the "back side" of it. He used to tell marvelous stories of what he had never seen. His narrations of imaginary puppies which we were to have if we were good boys, and vast quantities of maple sugar which some day or other perhaps would fall to our share, kept us awake for hours. He was a neat and talented fellow, having always an eye to the "main chance."

Cold shortened Johnny-cake was a compound intimately associated with my nursery life. It was baked on a board, and was made of flour instead of meal, with no leaven. Although slightly dyspep-

tic in its character, we all rose superior to its attacks. We were always hungry, and partook of it at unearthly hours. We would bite
it out into all manner of shapes, such as the heads of animals, birds,

and men. While we ate,
if not in bed, we never
kept still, but walked
about in procession, hop-
ping from one figure on
the carpet to another,
playing a game called
"Poison." This Johnny-
cake figured largely in
our morning bed-séances.
H. Auton rigged a pulley
on the top of the south-
west post of the big bed,
hitching it on the cur-
tain-hook and bringing
down the cords to be se-
cured around the back
of the high head-board.

To this apparatus was attached a basket, which H. Auton filled
with the precious Johnny-cake and hoisted to the mast-head, holding in his own hands, under his pillow, the governing ropes.

The contents of this mysterious pannier were to be lowered at
daylight, and administered to such individuals in the bed as the
autocrat should himself determine.

With the early dawn came a little rustling from all quarters of
the big bed and the jolly-boat. A ghostly procession of white forms

wended its way from all quarters. The trundle-bed gave up its little citizens. The front side and middle of the ark were all agog, the youthful crew climbing over the jaded anatomy of Deb'rah, and nestling down around the Johnny-cake owner with eager jaws. No sweet-bread or fillet of later years was ever so sweet as that little bit of cold, indigestible compound doled out to us on those dark and early mornings, as we sat, like savages, in our night-gowns, crouched around our Johnny-cake chief.

This primitive breakfast fitted us for an arduous journey "over the Andes," which we proceeded to do at once. There was a picture in one of our nursery books representing a long train of mules, laden with merchandise, toiling over the difficult passes of the Andes, and carrying to tide-water the produce of the country. This old wood-cut filled our youthful imaginations with a desire to act it out.

The girls and boys, with Ben Jackson, the negro, on hands and knees, in night-gowns and night-drawers, the oldest and biggest first, and then the little ones following on, with the black boy filling up the rear, would start from the southwest bed-post of the big bed, commencing at the top of the bolster on our trip over the mountains. Plunging under the bed-clothes we wriggled our way, one after the other, down to the bottom of the bed. Then we pulled away the ends of the blankets and the sheets down there, and wormed ourselves out from under these to the bottom-ends of the bed-clothes of the trundle-bed below. Then we passed up

through the whole length of these to the trundle-bed bolster, where we emerged, one after another, in a very disheveled condition. Taking breath at this big pillow, we continued our wearisome march over the outside of the little bed, mounted the foot of the ark, and pushed on to our first starting-point. For merchandise, we carried on our backs all the pillows we could get, the kitten and the puppy slung in handkerchiefs across our backs, and we presented quite a distressed and business-like appearance, as the long line of ruddy boys and girls, neighing and braying like horses and mules, would disappear and emerge at regular intervals from the stuffy bed-clothes.

Suddenly some new idea would strike the procession, when, presto! away flew puppy and kitten, up went the bed-clothes, out from all parts of the blankets would come white legs and night-gowns (the *disjecta membra* of Auton nursery), which came to a standstill before the wood fire.

There is little doubt but these expeditions thoroughly digested all the "shortened Johnny-cake," which we had consumed, and made us ravenous for the hot breakfast which Rosannah had been preparing in the kitchen below.

In Auton nursery was a famous stand made of oak, with a crack through the middle of its round top. This space was always filled with the remains of the soap and sand left by Deb'rah's scrubbing-brush, and which we used to pick out with pins. Around this modest bit of furniture we took our tea. It was an interesting and healthy sight to watch a bevy of girls and boys in high, checked aprons and ruffled collars, with red cheeks and shining curls, crim-

3

son, pouting lips and butter-teeth (as we used to call the second
set in front), chatting like magpies; all drinking, eating, and talking at once; all good-natured, happy, and uproarious. No political
questions disturbed our brains, no dictum of society divided our
councils. The shadow of the cow's foot in our milk and water was
the most serious object which attracted our attention, and a healthy

rivalry as to who could
bite out the greatest
number of the little
hearts from Mr. Co-
rey's cookies in a given
number of minutes
alone created excite-
ment. As the south-
west bed-post was the
famous starting-point
for all our imaginary
bed expeditions, so the
northeast one was the pole around which W. Auton, alias " Antelope," and Ben Jackson, the black boy, performed their celebrated
flying act. This circus-trick consisted in running from the bolster,
in stocking-feet, catching hold of the post with the left hand and
swinging completely about in a circle through the air, landing
on the bed again. Antelope and Ben were the two athletes of
the nursery, and were respected and obeyed accordingly. Against
these same bed-posts, also, the children pressed their oranges, after
reaming holes in them with their fore-fingers, preparatory to the
kneading and sucking process.

Our favorite nursery disease was sore throat. This malady enabled us to stay away from school and wear flannel about our necks ; yet we were not ill enough to leave off play, nor too ill to forego Malaga grapes and lemonade. It was an ailment possessing suffi-cient advantages to be prayed for, and the boy fortunate enough to have swollen tonsils was an ob-ject of envy. A croupy cough was another coveted disease. So desir-able was this that W. Auton per-suaded his younger sister to open the nursery window on a cold winter's day in order that he might hang his head out and "hoarsen up," as we called it.

These infantile devices often over-shot the mark, keeping us in bed for weeks. I owe a debt of gratitude, however, to raisins, which no amount of indigestion will ever eradicate. This fruit certainly made our path-way to knowledge an easier one, for those sudden stomach-aches, which were invented to come on about school-time, were imme-diately driven away by a small fat bunch of these grapes, together with a large greening apple stuffed into our pockets to eat at recess.

"leghorns," green veils, and old calashes that could be gathered
from the nursery-closet bandboxes, while wide lace collars and
stiff little "jiggers," made to fill out the mutton-legged sleeves of
our grandmother's dresses, were freely brought into requisition.
Enormous silk bags, and mother's scissors and pincushion, were hung
at the side, spectacles were put on nose, and old-fashioned mits
adorned the hands. To these were added wide pieces of different-
colored morocco, laced up over the wrists.

Mr and Mrs
John Monzy
and
"Almirah"
their eldest
daughter

"Old Buff," the family horse (A. Auton), was now led out from
the nursery-closet stable, where he had been browsing among the
medicines and eating his provender of pounded soda-cracker, and
sour "sorrel" pulled from the "upper garden." He neighed, and
whinnied, and stamped his feet on the children's toes, just like any

grown-up horse in the city. He kept off imaginary flies with his impromptu tail, made from a bundle of green lily-stalks pulled from the same upper-garden. A pair of bits made of pine wood were put in his mouth, and a string of jingly-jongly bells hung about his neck. A large dinner-bell was now put aboard the chairs which served for a family wagon, and the Honzys were ready to start. Tin kettles, toy pails, and other nursery utensils were freely brought into use to hold the imaginary huckle-berries, and thus equipped the signal was given to commence the journey. The horse began to trot up and down. The sleigh-bells started their jargon. The elder Honzys cried Whoa! and Get up! The younger Honzys screamed out that they already saw the fruit growing on every side. Ben Jackson, the black boy, dropped his hat, and had to get off and pick it up, while the neighbor's kitten, in its night-cap, mewed with delight at the expected huckle-berries. The old nursery floor rose and fell with the stamping and galloping. The air resounded with mews and screams. The big bell was continually ringing for people to " clear the track," while poor toothless Deb'rah was vainly beating the air, imploring us to " cease the racket." Such a babel brought its usual quietus in the forms of Mother and Father Auton, who appeared at the nursery door and commanded silence, — you might hear " a pin drop " in an instant.

This interruption was lucky, because the party had just arrived at the " berrying ground," and were already engaged in picking the largest specimens from all sides of the room. The pails were filled in " no time," and the family were at home again in " a twinkling." Somebody squeezed the kitten in the wrong place, which caused the neighbor's child to squall, leap from the flying vehicle, and rush under the trundle-bed with H. Auton's night-cap on, and its long,

black apron petticoat, half off, dragging behind it. The " cots "
and the " bandages " were flung to the four winds. The old toggery
was dropped on the floor for Deb'rah to pick up, while Mr. and Mrs.
Honzy lost their assumed authority at once, and mixed with demo-
cratic familiarity among their Auton brethren.

CHAPTER FIFTH.

ROOMS IN AUTON HOUSE.

STRANGE to tell. Auton House had but one bedroom. There were lots of other rooms, such as the "Green-room" and the "Dining-room" and the "Back and Front Drawing rooms," and the "Library," and the "Middle chamber," and the "White-room," and "Mother's room," and the "Baby-house," and "Rosannah's room," and the "boys' room," and "Fre'bun's room," and the "Glass-house," and the "Nursery," but only one "Bedroom." In this chamber all the strange new maids slept and got up early. It was as "cold as a barn," and had a fire-board in front of the fire-place with a painting upon it representing my father and uncle when children holding a steel-gray squirrel perched on their hands, and attached to a small chain of the same gray color dangling over their fingers. The boys wore large ruffled collars and roundabout jackets buttoned up to the throat, with their hair cut short in front, leaving it long behind. In this room, also, was a tall wicker basket which held soiled linen; W. Auton used to leap from the floor upon it, as far as the rim, where, see-sawing for a moment, he would pitch head-foremost into the depths below. This

bedroom opened out of the nursery, and was peeped into but
shunned by all the "young ones" as a haunted spot. It was so
near to our nursery paradise, yet such a poky locality, that these
two chambers stood in our vocabulary for the "good" and the

"wicked place." We peopled
this latter neighborhood, with all
those dreadful characters which
disturbed our infant imaginations,
and shuddered lest at that very
instant that gloomy abode might
conceal a horrid creature, known
to all the children by the name of
"Bloody-bones," who went about
killing babies and hiding their
bodies under the sand-hill in the
rear of Aunt Malbone's house.
There were connected with each
of the chambers in Auton House
most delightful and pleasing asso-
ciations. With the little Green-room in particular these associa-
tions were especially charming. In it were concentrated all the
wit and frolic of Auton House. On Sunday evenings the pleasant-
est set of people gathered there. On either side the broad hearth
sat our parents — the dearest, the funniest, the most congenial of
spirits. My father Auton reclined in the great arm-chair, close by
the long window, out of which one of his hot hands was always
hung to cool, while he puffed his aromatic cigar, and recounted to
us his wonderful story, of being shut up in a tomb when he was a
boy, and of his playing a tune upon the great iron doors with the

thigh-bones which he found scattered about him. As the evening wore on in trooped his favorite nephews, Ned and Ben, William and George, Can and Levi, to smoke the Sunday pipe. To these were added a large detachment of home production, and the "younger fry" from the nursery completed the family party. The air was full of fragrant smoke (which some folks dislike). The sputtering fire sent forth its cheerful blaze. The round convex mirror, with its black dragons and gilded sconces, reflected the genial brightness, while the flickering light on the "Bear picture," "The Marriage of The Virgin," "The Two Mackerel," and "The Horatii and the Curatii," completed a scene of comfort and good cheer. These evenings began with a bountiful tea. The family was so large, however, that we "kids" were kept in check in the nursery until the older parties had finished. Listening and giggling at the top of the stairs, we awaited the signal to descend. Then, whooping and shouting, sliding on balusters, three steps at a time, while poor Deb'rah was beseeching us to make less noise, the invading host came thundering down to tea. Fish-balls, brown-bread toast, hot biscuits, baked beans, Indian pudding, and quince marmalade vanished before these hungry Philistines as quickly as a western wheat field succumbs to the advance of the caterpillar. That it was possible to pack into a child's stomach, holding a pint, more than enough to fill a quart, was beautifully demonstrated whenever an empty

Auton boy came within hail of any article in the above category.
A "symposium of smoke" was instituted in the little Green-room
after tea. The hospitable front door constantly admitted some fresh
addition to the genial company — either "Tris," who hitched

"Katie in the chaise" at the tree-
box, or kind friends from "over the
bridge," increased the number of
welcome guests. Auton nursery was
now drawn upon to furnish amusement. One boy spoke "On Linden
when the sun was low" with so
much gesticulation and fervor that
it was dangerous to go near him.
Another one drew the forms of animals in the air at lightning speed,
and with so many flourishes and cur-
licues that the company kept themselves at a respectful distance from
his revolving fist. The youngest
of all, with hair sticking up like a
feather-duster, whistled cleverly
quite difficult airs, keeping time with his fingers on the door-panel,
which he used for a drum; while still another cut with scissors, from
black paper, capital likenesses of the company in the shortest possible time. After these harmless performances candles were brought,
and we all repaired to the drawing-room to sing psalm tunes, after
the ancient New England fashion. The old organ had stood in this
room so long that it seemed to be a relation of the family. It had
a fluted front of flowered cherry damask, which is as intimately as-

sociated with my boyhood as was Aunt Moody's stubbed thumb, or Deb'rah's scanty front hair which we had combed almost out of her head. The organ had also a crowd of funny ivory stops, labeled "Tutti" and "Haut-boy" and "Reed," which squeaked and talked to us in a most familiar manner, and which we regarded much in the same sort of friendly way as we looked upon the boys in the neighborhood who used to come into our yard to play with us. The Tutti stop in particular always made us laugh, the name was such a queer one. One of the girls "presided" at the instrument, while a little boy "blew." "We don't want any coatee tunes," said Father Auton; "give us a good long-waister." There is a smack of seriousness suggested by the devotional swing and dignified rhythm of such old-fashioned airs as "Bangor" and "Denmark," which communicated itself to the assembly. "All hail the power of Jesus' name" was always given with effect, the whole strength of the company being expended on the oft-repeated chorus, "And crown him Lord of all." Also the last line in the first verse of "Ye Christian heroes," "And plant the rose of Sharon there." This was never sung without a visible quaver in Father Auton's voice as he sat, with closed eyes, his hands clasped across his ample figure. . . .

Mother Auton was subject to what we children called "spazzums." These were in reality severe attacks of dyspepsia, and would seize her suddenly at the breakfast-table with but little premonition. The pain was so intense as to nearly stop her breath, and while it continued she was always in a critical condition. We children could tell when these attacks approached by noticing her nostrils, which were slightly distended when suffering from pain

she wished to conceal. "There!" we would say to each other.
"mother's going to have a spazzum; don't you see how her nostrils stick out?"

Once fastened upon her, these spazzums never let go until Dr.
Possett had poured down McMunn's Elixir by the table-spoonful.
Every stitch of clothing had to be loosened while Deb'rah, and
Rosannah, and father, and the new girl, and our older sisters rubbed
and rubbed the "small of her back" until the skin was almost
rubbed away. We children, frightened to death, congregated in
the upper entry, and inquired of every passer-by if "mother
would n't die?" Some of us burst into tears, while others said
they "felt" as much as we did, but "were n't going to cry about
it." The weaker ones used to repair to the lonely, back drawing-
room to pray in the dark that the spazzum might pass off. How
strange it is, that with this recollection comes another, equally
vivid, but just as quaint as the former one was sad. It is the peculiar odor of the black hair-cloth seating of the mahogany chair
where we knelt to offer our petition. That queer, half-musty, half-
hairy, varnishy perfume is as distinct in my recollection as is the
melancholy occasion which bowed my head upon it. These sudden
attacks terribly afflicted our tender-hearted father. I can see him
plainly at this moment flying about with anxious countenance and
wild expression, tumbling over chairs and slamming doors as he
rushed up and down stairs for alcohol, salt, or hot water.

On one lugubrious morning when Mother Auton was groaning,
and the whole household was rubbing her for "dear life," a favorite
spaniel belonging to T. Auton took it into his head to have a fit, and
flew around the dining-room at a terrible rate, foaming at the mouth,
etc. Just at this juncture Father Auton appeared at the dining-

room door; and seeing the dog covered with saliva, floundering
and kicking under his feet, while all the children were watching
him from the tops of tables and chairs; he became transfixed with
emotion. At last he shouted at the top of his voice, " D—n it!
was ever a mortal so put upon? Wife dying up-stairs — mad-dog
down — get out ! "

Happily neither of these direful calamities happened: both our
mother and the spaniel speedily recovered, but what Father Auton
screamed out on this occasion was never forgotten.

CHAPTER SIXTH.

THE MIDDLE CHAMBER.

HE middle chamber possessed the rare dignity of being the spot where nearly every Auton first saw the light. There was an odor of new flannel and powder-puff about it which never quite departed, while a depressing stillness pervaded the apartment on those periodic occasions when we children were allowed to view the last "newcomer" from an unknown country.

The "fresh Auton" was carried, for its primal bath, into a small adjoining room called the "Library." Here Miss Betsey Arnold held the struggling stranger gently on her lap while the long file of girls and boys from the nursery marched in to pass judgment upon it. "What a nose!" "He looks like a monkey." "Look what a face it's making." "He's the ugliest baby I ever saw," etc. These ingenuous remarks were the unbiased opinions pronounced upon every new Auton as it appeared. They say that "children and fools speak the truth." The middle chamber was also the room which our big brother occupied when he came home on a visit. He always arrived by the boat train which reached the city at four o'clock in the morning. We children, who held him in great veneration, never caught sight of him on such visits until breakfast time, when he sedately descended in his slippers to read the morning paper in quiet reserve. He was his "mother's hope," and his "father's joy," — and well he might be, for he was held up before us as an example of everything that was noble and worthy of imitation — so the chamber had to be well aired before he came. It seems but yesterday that all these preparations were going on. Mother Auton in the cold room clearing out the drawers to make way for J. Auton's underclothes, the company pin-cushion hauled out and put in place under the mirror, the best comb and brush laid in a convenient spot for use, and the blue china pitchers filled with the pump-water. Oftentimes, at early dawn, we could hear the creak of the carriage wheels when the vehicle stopped before the house, and the thud of his trunk upon the sidewalk. He frequently roused up Deb'rah by rattling the blinds

in the back yard with a clothes-pole to let him in; but Mother Auton generally anticipated any such manœuvre, and greeted her son even before the hack-man had gotten upon his box. From our snug quarters in the big bed we could hear the dull boom of the heavy front door as it shut again, then a little desultory undertoned conversation, a pair of boots dropped on the outside of his apartment, and all was quiet. The middle chamber was also the

"spare room," set apart for invited guests at Auton House. Here

4

Mr. and Mrs. McLacken slept when they paid us a visit from New Haven. Mr. McLacken had a neck so thin and long that it required folds upon folds of cravat to build it up to the standard size of ordinary necks. He was always on a strict diet, and was constantly going up-stairs to take his medicine. Here reposed blonde Cousin Fanny, and tired Theodore, who had a very long upper lip and went to sleep in his chair every evening; and here rested Cousin John, who had a Roman nose and chafed his hands together whenever he met you; and sprightly Cousin Maria with her beaming smile and her flying cap-strings.

These cousins were all from Boston, where they had the enormous frog-pond, and ice-creams so large that no boy could eat any more than from the top of one of " them " as far down as the rim of the glass. They had Boston trunks, owned Boston chaises, ate Boston cream-cakes from Mrs. Meyers', and " took " " Boston Transcripts." They drank " cambric tea," and ate stale bread, and when they spoke of what was going on in their city they said " with us," all the time.

Our big brother remarked that it did n't matter what our cousins ate or drank, or what forms of expression they used, so long as they had " public spirit " which we in our town did n't have "a spec of." We did n't dare ask what " public spirit " meant; but among ourselves concluded that it had reference to some sort of liquor which the Boston Mayor drank.

Cousin Fannie wore caps with lots of ribbons, and gave us sugared flag-root which stung our stomachs.

The middle chamber also enjoyed the privilege of being the apartment where the ladies took off their " things " when we had a party. Its mahogany bed-posts were elaborately ornamented with carved pine-apples and their spiked leaves. The red silk curtains about the bed and windows had a deep fringe of tassels and balls, and the pillow-cases and bed-linen were the best that Anton House afforded. But for all that the room smelt strange and had a prim, shut-up, visitor-like air about it. A picture of Ariadne left on the sea-shore and waiting for her clothes hung just over the pier-glass. My grandfather's and grandmother's portraits looked steadily down from the walls, and kept in awe any little boy or girl who dared to talk above a whisper.

The deep mahogany wardrobe, made by Josey Rawson, and reaching to the ceiling, contained within its ample bosom the party gowns, the old lace, the ancient fur boas, and the high "leghorn hats" of my mother. And here rested the tall Canton jars which came from China in the "Ann and Hope," and which "once upon a time" were filled with Canton rock candy with white strings running through it. When the silver branches shed their mellow radiance around the middle chamber, and the bright firelight danced over the newly-scoured brasses, and the room got thoroughly warmed up, it presented a genial and comfortable appearance, — that is, for an apartment set apart as this was from all the rest; but we children kept clear of it, for it always seemed to be saying to us, "Tread lightly, children, I am the spare-room!" On state occasions the middle chamber was at "its best." Deb'rah and the maid had hardly finished their folding, and dusting, and putting away, before the door-bell commenced ringing, and word was passed from mouth to mouth in the nursery, "The company's come!" "The company's come!"

The emotions which rambled up and down my bosom at such junctures cannot be described. Faint photographs of them, how-

ever, have visited me, from time to time, since my boyhood, as I
have listened to the bright uproar of some "grown-up" ball-room.

I used to be in such an excited state that Deb'rah would have to
dress me up before dark.

The new suit, just home from Aunt Nancy Miller's, with its brass

buttons, and broad,
ruffled collar, was
buttoned up and
pinned down before
sunset. Hands
were washed (a bad
job well over), and
hair smoothed, if
such a thing was
possible with a tan-
gled mass of yel-
low tow full of
"widows' peaks"
and "cow-licks."
As soon as possible
I sprang from the
nursery, first down
to the front door,
where black Fre'bun stood in white cotton gloves, and a pointed,
woolly tuft like a steeple on the top of his head. Then I sped
through the two drawing-rooms which were being lighted, then
slyly peeped into the supper-room, only to be driven out by Rosannah and Mother Auton, who were surveying the tables for the last
time. Then up the front stairs like a shot, through my mother's

room, where the wood fire had fallen down, then round by the third
story stairs, down the upper hall and into the middle chamber.
Here I stopped, breathless. The "company" had, indeed, appeared
in the shape of two old "goodies" who made it a point to arrive
on the notch of time, and had already deposited their "things" on
the bed.

While Deb'rah adjusted their rumpled gowns they surveyed the
staring boy before them, and then remarked: "Why, C. Anton,
don't you know us? I'm Cousin Mary, and I am Cousin Sephronia."
Then they turned to each other, and one of them said, "He's a
bright boy, but I can't say he's handsome." "This is their spare-
room, these are Governor and Mrs. Tones's portraits, the carpet is a
good deal faded, ain't it? but the sheets, I see, are all linen. Look
at that horrid picture behind the pier-glass! It is positively indecent.
I suppose they put it in here out of the way of the children." "We
shall have an elegant supper, because they know all about what
good eating is in this house. Mr. Anton is a perfect epicure, you
know!" "They allow the children to eat everything." "Come!
let's go down." "I'm ready!" "Does my petticoat show?"

These two old ladies, of course, had no idea that I had understood
every bit of their conversation, and had detailed it, word for word,
within five minutes afterwards, to the little inquisitive ears in the
nursery. Then I commenced my racing again; first into the third
story, where my brothers were dressing, then down again to the
drawing-room, sliding on the banisters half the way on my new
jacket, and scraping the varnish with my brass buttons the whole
length, besides losing one of my "pumps" in the descent.

I watched my opportunity, and when nobody observed I stole
into the darkened supper-room again to sniff the condiments I was

not allowed to eat. What delicious odors were wafted into my nostrils as I entered there ! The first sniff revealed a fragrant mélange of calf's-foot jelly, and joggly blanc-mange. Then a creamy, winey, fruity fragrance was given off from the tall glass pyramid of whips and soft custards, first a whip, then a custard, then a whip, then a custard, interspersed with Malaga grapes and sparkling jelly. Fat raisins and blanched almonds lay intermingled in delightful abundance, while mountains of " hearts and rounds " (each with its slice of citron, and of my mother's own make) were piled on the silver cake-baskets at the corners. The heavy decanters rested in their silver holders. The ponderous cut-glass bowl held aloft its precious burden of salad, while vacant-places at either end of the table remained for the oysters and terrapin. Wine-glasses were piled together in silver baskets. Forks and spoons lay huddled in delicious profusion on every hand, while antique salvers and quaint little basins held the confectionery we called " sentiments," and the " short " biscuits.

As I stood there musing, I could but think how few the fleeting moments would be before that mountain of lolly-pops and joy would be gone forever. Those fleecy whips guzzled by strangers, and the " hearts and rounds " (deprived of their citron) all wasted and broken. I stole just one prune, and put the tip of my finger into the " floating island " to see how it tasted, and then hurriedly closing the door commenced again the " grand rounds " of the rooms.

On such great occasions the children were sent to bed before supper was served, with the promise of their plate of " good things " the next morning.

These were brought to us before we quitted the warm blankets of the ark and the trundle-bed. In the middle of the plate usually stood a tall whip, the bubbles of which, weary of standing up, had quietly collapsed into a dried creamy film. About the whip were grouped a yellow soft custard, a piece of trembling blanc-mange, specked with little particles of almond shells which lay in the immediate vicinity, one five-fingered piece of preserved ginger, the syrup of which had run under the bottom of the whip-glass and stuck the same to the plate. A heap of raisins, two figs, one "heart and round," one glass of calf's-foot jelly, three or four "sentiments," with "tells" rolled up in them, and four prunes.

The prospect of these "good things" made us hail with delight every one of Mother Auton's parties. Once, on a cold December night when the thermometer was at zero, and the carriage-wheels creaked on the snow, occurred quite an exciting event. The back drawing-room fire-place was piled up with logs to multiply the heat. There was neither gas nor furnace in those days, and people had to rely upon hickory wood and wax candles for bodily comfort. The great halls of houses were "cold as Greenland." Everybody's back was "goose-flesh," while everybody's face was red-hot. That night in particular the wood was piled up, and its yellow glare shot out into every portion of the drawing-room. I remember among the company a beautiful Southern lady who

wore a crimson velvet gown trimmed with white lace, and owned
lots of darkies. Suddenly there was a cry of "fire!" The wood-
work in the middle chamber, just above us, had ignited from the
heat of the chimney below. There was an immediate commotion
among the fair dames and lordly cavaliers, who rushed up the front
stairway in order to save the ladies' wraps, — their green silk calashes,
and ungainly "india-rubbers," their long yarn stockings to draw
over the silk ones, and their satin-wadded pelisses, — which were piled
up in elegant confusion on the middle chamber bed. There was

only a voluntary fire department in
those days. Every boy's father was
either a "fire-ward" or a captain in
the bucket-brigade; so when the
alarm was sounded the old leathern
buckets which hung in the "glass-
house" were snatched from their
fastenings and brought into immediate requisition.

Beautiful women, with jeweled fingers and dresses tucked back, stood
on the front stairs passing buckets,
while a band of "swells" in white
kids (white kids were then fashionable) worked the kitchen-pump,
and slopped the water over the brussels carpets. It was a pictur-
esque and lively scene for some time.

Happily the conflagration was arrested, and everybody enjoyed
the hot supper which followed this excitement all the more. There
was no need that year for the services of the little woolly-headed
chimney-sweep, who so regularly shinned up the big-throated flues

to scrape down their sooty sides, and his melodious carol was piped in the crisp morning air from the topmost stone of our neighbor's smoke-stack.

T. Auton owned a white "Cade" lamb. This animal wore a red morocco collar, and followed its master about the streets.

> "Everywhere T. Auton went
> The lamb was sure to go."

It became, however, a great nuisance. Its nose was everywhere but in its proper place, no marble mantel-piece, nor mahogany bedstead, were too high for it to scale: indeed, it seemed to choose these delicate pieces of furniture for its especial landing-places. Its idiotic "baa" was heard everywhere, and its hot, woolly presence was quite too much on long summer days.

Besides the lamb, T. Auton had a poodle. "Carlo" had no tail, but nature made up the deficiency to him by his unusual sagacity, and the pity he excited among men on account of this deprivation. His eyes were red, as if from weeping. He sat down before every new-comer, placed his paw in his lap, and looked up to him with his red eyes, as if to invoke his pity. "Carlo has no tail," he seemed to say, "He can only wriggle the end of his back-bone when he feels happy, only that and nothing more."

This call for sympathy affected everybody, and all the children

in particular were his firm friends. So Carlo, or, as Rosannah the
cook called him, Carla, and the lamb, and T. Auton, and the rocking-horse on the piazza were four inseparables.

The lamb would "baa," and Carla would bark, and T. Auton would
scamper round the yard playing horse, and switching his impromptu tail (made out of green lily-stalks, or of his own pocket-
handkerchief), while the old rocking-horse grinned, and stared at

his three friends with his
glass eye from off the piazza. On one of these
party occasions above al-
luded to, the supper-table
was elaborately set. The
window-shutters in the
banqueting hall were
closed. All things were
ready for serving the feast.
The best china and the cut-
glass dishes stood in re-
spectable positions amidst
the family silver. Rosannah the cook had carefully brought in the
joggling jelly and the flubbering "floating island." Our mother

had surveyed the scene and pronounced it one of her very best "set tables," when, Baa! baa! and in rushed the lamb, leaped on the table, galloped around among the soft custards, and the pre-served ginger, poked his nose into the jelly, paused to browse on the chicken-salad, and sniffed at the "hearts and rounds." Then he stooped and baa'd again, as if to say: "There is some mistake about this. Evidently this is not the table-land for me to nibble." All this time Mother Anton and black Rosannah stood aghast. The old cook opened her eyes and hardly dared to breathe, while Mother Anton shut hers, and hardly dared to stop breathing; each expecting to hear the fatal crash, for should that napkin bowl, brought from China in 1812, be broken, or that great cut-glass dish which Aunt Cutler had given to

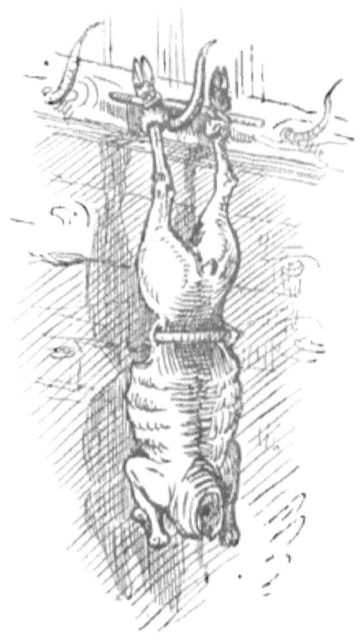

Grandmother Dunn, be shattered by that "horrid sheep," they never could be replaced. Meanwhile the "precious lamb" picked his way among wine-glasses and English walnuts, and beat a hasty retreat without oversetting a salt-cellar or disturbing a cracker.

This escapade, however, settled his "hash," for not many days afterwards the red collar was taken off his neck, and his neck was taken off his body, and his body was taken off the premises. So the Cade lamb was no more.

CHAPTER SEVENTH.

WORK AND PLAY.

LOVE for drawing was a marked characteristic among the Auton boys. Deb'rah used to say that we got it from our "father's side," whatever that expression might mean; we stimulated it by constant exercise, so that it became a source of intense enjoyment. A habit of observation resulted in great facility of expression, which converted Auton nursery into an infant drawing-school. The delineation of figures was our especial hobby, so that whenever a new drawing-book came into our possession we immediately set to work on some favorite beast, generally a horse. We drew his ears first because this gave us time to decide, as we proceeded, whether he should be running away or only in the stable. A favorite way we had was to sit in little chairs, all in a row, with our slates on our knees, and see who could draw the best lion or the fastest trotter. These sketches, when completed, were submitted to our older brothers for judgment. Sometimes Father Auton would visit the nursery, and with his great thumb rub out the forelegs of our favorite horse, telling us that we "never saw a leg crooked-up in that way; it was all wrong,

and we must try again." So away we
went to work once more, and with better
results.

In these friendly bouts we discovered
the secret of making a horse look as if
he were actually moving along the road.
We found that motion could not be in-
dicated unless all the legs of the animal
were off the ground at once, and that
the moment any part of him touched
the earth this idea of motion ceased.
We tried in all sorts of ways to prove
this. We got down upon our hands and
knees and trotted about the nursery
floor. We sat at the window listening
to the sound of a horse trotting on the
cobble-stones. We watched the animals
in every possible position as they sped

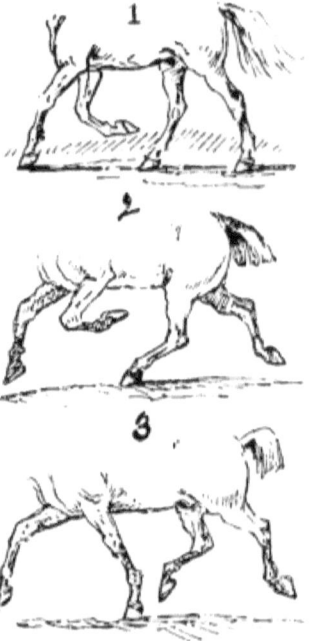

by us, to detect some point of time when all four legs were off the
ground at once.
After many
weary watchings
we settled the
question in the
affirmative, so
that Auton nurs-
ery became the

last court of appeal on all trotting questions.

This practice of observation was valuable to us in a variety of

ways. For instance, in order to catch the correct movement of a
tiger dispatching his victim. Deb'rah would allow us to take our
beefsteak and our cutlets out of our plates down on the nursery-
floor. Here, crouching over our imaginary hunter or expiring buf-
falo between our paws, we tore off great pieces of his flesh from
the bone, and, raising aloft our defiant but greasy visages, swallowed the morsel without mastication.

In this way we caught what we called the " feel " of the tiger,
and could thus impart to our representation of him a greater
amount of snarl and ferocity. Then, again, in the same manner,
by constant practice we could imitate the proud walk of a rooster
among the hens. We scratched up imaginary Easter-worms, we
cocked our heads from side to side, as if our eyes were on our tem-
ples. We flapped our arms and crew from the backs of chairs and
imaginary hen-coops, and pecked at fancied pullets that presumed
to come too near our harem. Thus we imbibed something of that
" inner consciousness " of an ordinary red rooster, which enabled

us to draw him out on the slate so vividly that one could almost
hear him crow. The natural result of this artistic diathesis were
moving dioramas, stuffed elephants, living tableaux and private
theatricals. On the evenings of such exhibitions, our sisters were
stationed at the confectionery table, where diminutive sticks of
candy were sold for a cent apiece to our long-suffering audience,
who sat for our sakes on the hardest kind of boards in Egyptian
darkness for two mortal hours. The fund realized from this source
was expended in blue cambric and paste-board for the Diorama.

F. Anton carved with his jack-knife the little wooden automata
which figured in the different scenes. Bill Paine was the magician
who appeared in the interludes and swallowed fire, while H. Anton
manipulated the strings which set in motion the dioramic world.
One of our scenes represented a cobbler's shop. The curtain rose.
The shoemaker sat at his bench pegging his shoe. A knock was
heard at the door. The old fellow raised his head and asked the
stranger to walk in. The door opened, a well-dressed individual
entered who asked to have his shoe mended. Up went his leg to
exhibit the rent. The cobbler inspected it, and said he would patch
it the next day. Down went the leg. Right about went the
stranger. The door flew open and he disappeared, whereupon the
cobbler dropped his head and commenced pegging away again at
his shoe, and the scene ended amid the plaudits of the audience
hidden in the cimmerian darkness above alluded to. Afterwards
came a tiger-scene in South Africa, and a blacksmith shop on the
road to Pomfret, and a pasteboard naval battle in the War of 1812;
and enough more wonderful things fully worth the price of admis-
sion, which was five cents. We used to print and sell the tickets
for these dioramas weeks before we had done the first thing to the

exhibition itself. The advantage of this arrangement was that quite
often the affair never came off, and yet the buyers of our tickets
scarcely ever consented to take back their cash. This was a mean
trick of ours to make money, but the idea must have been put into
our heads by those strange boys who came into our yard and were
forever begging to "belong." This word, translated, meant to
become one of the proprietors of the company, having a right

to a full share in the profits without
doing any of the work. It was a
wonderful sight to creep under the
gay drapery which concealed the ma-
chinery of our exhibition, and view
the spot where H. Auton pulled that
wilderness of strings which set in
motion the little world above him.
One small smoky lamp from the
kitchen stood in the corner and shed
a flickering light around. A tangled
web of threads with labels attached
to the ends hung from little holes

over his head. One string went to the old cobbler's arm, another
lifted the stranger's leg. This one made the Bengal tiger spring
at the native, and that pulled down the main-mast of the Guer-
rière, shot away by the brave boys in the Constitution; and so
on, through all the scenes. H. Auton sat on a little cricket with
his legs crossed and his head bent back, studying the forest of
threads above him. Great drops of perspiration stood on his upper
lip and dropped off his chin. He breathed an atmosphere which
would have suffocated anybody but a boy or an Esquimaux, and

he emerged from his lair after each performance parboiled, but happy. Some of these dioramas ended in our foreign proprietors getting suddenly mad and leaving the yard *en masse*. Once in a while also Al' Young and Nic' Peters (those naughty Meeker Street boys!) would blow out the only light at the confectionery table, and decamp with all the candy and the pasteboard money. These little *contretemps*, however, were neither anticipated nor feared by us younger ones, as we sat, with eyes like saucers, in exquisite expectancy, watching for the green curtain to raise its mysterious front.

5

CHAPTER EIGHTH.

OUR MOTHER AUTON.

 IF a boy expects to enter this world at all, he has got to have some kind of a mother, but then there were only seven boys who had my mother for their mother. One of the few things left to me, nowadays, which gives me unalloyed satisfaction, is the fact that I had my mother for a mother. If I had some other boy's mother, knowing the good things that I do about my own mother, I shouldn't have been contented. Somehow she seemed different from Ed Gould's mother, for instance (the boy who bit the caterpillar in two), and yet, I presume, in many respects, she was much the same as the ordinary run of mothers. We boys always knew what Mother Auton would do on certain occasions. There was no cheating about her. When she said, "I'll see," we knew just as well that we should have what we were begging her for, as if she had actually said, "Yes, my dear, you may have it." When we had fever turns, the touch of her cool, soft hands on our brows was better than any spirits of nitre that Dr. Possett gave us to bring down the pulse; and when we snuggled up to her motherly

bosom, we slept more sweetly than on any other pillow. In later life, how puzzled grandfather would have been, to span her portly waist with his two hands, as he used to do so easily when she was but eighteen! and to look into her sweet blue eyes no one would detect the hidden "snap" which lay there, and which manifested itself, too, when we tried her patience beyond a certain limit. When she spanked us she lost her breath, the blows were so short and rapid, and, dear soul! the punishment injured her more than it did us, for we went off to our corners saying, "Didn't hurt us any!" while she was pale with excitement and exhausted from her encounter. Old-fashioned and dignified, delightful in conversation, and loved by everybody, elegant in her manners and an angel in sickness, my mother Auton was a "jewel and a love."

Our grandfather was a prominent Federalist in the State, and after the War of 1812 became its Governor, and his daughter was naturally an important factor in the gubernatorial mansion. The habitual reception and entertainment of strangers beget a certain ease and self-possession which few other things impart, and I well remember the grace with which she entered the drawing-room and courtesied to some person who had called upon her. It was that quaint, old-fashioned courtesy, half coy, half formal, which survived the Revolutionary period, and charmed everybody. The children thought her a grand performer on the piano. She was a favorite pupil of old blind Oliver Shaw, the music teacher, and when she sat at the instrument and commenced the "Battle of Prague" for us, we stood about the piano with heads just tall enough to view the key-board, and eyes and ears wide open with delight. As her fingers undulated up and down the scales we could see the advance of the troops, and hear the rattling of the musketry, the cries of the wounded, and the groans of the dying, almost as distinctly as if the actual battle was before us. When the performance ended it left us in a cold perspiration.

The "Infant Boys of Switzerland" was another favorite piece, and also, "Come rest in this bosom, my own stricken deer!" The cross-hand movement in this last composition we considered the most wonderful of all. That she should never miss striking the correct note with the middle finger of one hand stretched across the other was the marvel of marvels. Whenever afterwards we prac-

ticed the piano on the nursery tables and baby-chairs, this cross-hand manœuvre was the object we all tried to attain.

Mother Auton was a "Lady Bountiful" in the old-fashioned sense. She lived at an epoch when hospitality was a Christian virtue, and a stranger became a member in a man's own household. "Full measure, heaped up and running over," was the invisible legend engraven over her blessed heart, and she turned her face from no poor man at the door. All the colored people squatted to her in the street, and "Minty Weeks," Zip Brinturn's wife, Vi'lette Jackson and "Aunty ———," in mob caps, checked aprons, silver-bowed spectacles, and big india-rubber shoes, would wend their noiseless way through the upper entry to her chamber-door, to pour into her patient and sympathetic ear their worn-out tales of "rheumatiz" and "gone feelin's." These groanings were sure to be relieved by potions of "spirits," and remnants of old flannel, dealt out to them from that inexhaustible store, always on hand, somewhere in the "baby-house" closet.

There were a few occasions when Mother Auton's disapprobation was strangely excited. She called women who were guilty of anything derogatory to their sex "impudent hussies" and "saucy trollops;" and old men who paraded about the hot streets on Fourth of Julys with masonic aprons, and compasses on their stomachs, "stupid asses." She considered Dr. McGee and Dr. Eben Cowen the greatest physicians in the world. She hung little bags of camphor about the children's necks in the time of "the cholera." She "cleaned house" in the first week of May, rain or shine, and took such pride in her "boys" that it would have "fairly killed her" had any one of them gone amiss. Now all these qualities made her an ideal maternal relative.

Her nose was large, which we didn't object to, and her stature was tall, which just balanced her nose. She wore a cap, the strings of which were tied just between the chin she was born with and the other one she acquired with age. This made it very convenient for the strings, which never budged from their position. We used to like to have her come into the nursery and sing to us her favorite lullaby. —

"Rumpty Toodle — he was there!
Tittery, Nan, and Tarey O.," etc.

And when she reached the last line of the poem —

"Fall down, Daddy O — O — O — O,"

which was repeated on several soft keys, and in the minuendo scale, we all slipped off to the land of dreams with smiles on our lips, and faces cuddled up under her dear double chin.

It was our delight to pick the first raspberries of the season which grew in the "upper garden," and bring them to her in little sau-

cers. We all gathered about her knee to watch her eat them. She took each one up on the point of a pin in the daintiest manner, dipped it into the sugar we brought her, and dropped it into her mouth like a lady that she was. For our sakes (who had picked them for her) she ate the bad and the good ones,— those that tasted of rose-bugs, and those that were covered with white-wash off the trellis. Should a single berry, however inferior, escape her observation, we stood ready to remind her of it. "There! mother, you have n't eaten that little green one!" Sometimes she really could not eat such poor-looking specimens, whereupon we (who were dying to swallow the whole of them) cleared the little saucers in the twinkling of an eye.

The age of letter-writing is past. The era of Madame de Sévigne and Madame de Staël is buried beneath the rush of modern civilization. But there was a period when it was the fashion to

write letters and to express one's self on paper in cultivated diction.
This was the age of Chesterfield and of the "Tattler." Men and
women cultivated conversation as an art, and struggled for the mas-
tery of expression at the pen's point.

Mother Auton was bred in that spirit, and matured under the
influence of that past generation. Her ideas flowed as easily as
water, and her nimble pen posted them in black and white with as-
tonishing facility, even after eighty winters had passed over her
head.

What a correspondent she was, to be sure! "Wait for Mother
Auton's letters, if you want to hear the truth about it!" was the
common shibboleth in the family. Her epistles were comforts to
the homesick school-boy, the delight of her children in foreign
lands, and became valuable transcripts of the current history of
the whole Auton tribe. For forty years she wrote a weekly bulle-
tin to her absent ones, bringing to their anxious hearts fresh photographs of home.

Mother Auton never would sit at a desk. Neither "secretary"
nor "davenport" suited her purpose. The little gifts presented
to her from time to time, and admirably adapted to write at, were
always gratefully accepted, but never used. She took her writing
materials on her broad, motherly lap, pushed her cap-strings from her
face, adjusted her gold spectacles over her ample nose, dipped her
pen daintily in the ink (just enough to fill it without blotting), and
away it ran so merrily and easily over the paper that she would be
on her fourth page before we children, who were seated around her,
had half gotten through sucking our oranges. People write letters
now, lots of them, heaps of them; but I very much doubt whether
they contain one half the valuable news, — the harmless gossip, the
genial spirit, which flowed so readily from Mother Auton's pen.

There she sat in her chair every Sunday morning for over forty years, writing the weekly epistle, with bended head and benign expression, while the wood fire hissed and sputtered, and the old canary sang in the sun-light.

CHAPTER NINTH.

LL children are queer, and why should n't they be? It is no more than natural that such little pieces of animated putty should exhibit some extraordinary peculiarities before they become acquainted with their new existence. Just peep at a fresh-born baby and notice what disproportion there is between brain and body! Infants are not much more than tadpoles with possibilities. A soft rounded mass of brain-matter with a disproportionate appendage of soft bones. Sometimes the nutriment given these embryotic people stimulates the brain at the expense of the bones, and sometimes contrariwise. From this inequality of nutrition spring abnormal results. One small specimen is all head, while another is little else than stomach. And this unequal development often continues with their growth.

The Auton children were no exceptions to this state of things. We had our peculiarities like other folks, and like all other families we had a "young one" in ours who articulated sentences long before it ought to have done so. It bawled out "That's my baby — give me a cracker!" at so tender an age that Mother Auton screamed for Dr. Possett at once ; but Father Auton pooh-poohed the idea, saying that " it was all right, it was only a girl."

Then we always carried our stockings to bed and put them behind our pillows, and that was rather an odd habit. Besides that, we used to say our prayers on the front stairs in the middle of the day, so as to save time at night when we were sure to be so sleepy. This was a business-like habit, but a very naughty one. We all had what Dr. Possett called "chronic exaltation of the imagination," and saw dragons' heads and demons' faces in the air after we were abed. We discovered all kinds of animals in the yellow grain of the Egyptian marble mantel-piece in the green room, and in the dying embers of the fire. We lay on the floor pressing in our eyeballs with our fists, in order to enjoy afterwards those gorgeous and changing figures produced on the retina by the pressure. We had also an inconvenient way of suddenly waking from sleep in the greatest trepidation, and screaming for Deb'rah. This succeeded in arousing the house, but to our great cost ; because our exasperated parents, seeing that we were screaming for nothing, made us finish our hullaballoo by screaming for something. — this Mother Auton administered to us in a very rapid but effective manner.

When T. Auton was a little boy he was so frightened because Charley Arnold threatened to put him in a pin-hole in the fence that he did n't get over it for years ; and the tradition is that F. Auton was never able to go church because when the minister said " Kingdom come " it made him so terribly ill that he was obliged to leave the pew. This same F. Auton was uncomfortably affected by circuses, for the moment the brass band "struck up" he left the tent, saying that he "*felt the bass-drum in his stomach.*"

The Auton children were in mortal fear of telling a lie, and in their circumlocution to avoid a falsehood they generally contrived to tell one. They used to say " they did n't know " when they did

know, and " believed " this thing to be so when they knew all about
it. The whole of Auton nursery expected inevitably to die before
morning unless each night somebody who knew about such things
assured it to the contrary. One evening T. Auton sent his younger
sister down-stairs to settle this important point for him, while he
awaited the verdict in his night-drawers on the top step. The com-

pany gathered in the " green-
room " were startled by seeing
the door open, and a little girl
in long white night-gown and
ruffled cap enter. She strode
solemnly up to Mother Auton
and in serious tones said, " T.
Auton wants to know if he will
live till morning." Everybody
was convulsed with laughter,
but it was no laughing matter
to the lassie who performed
her task with imperturbable
gravity, and then marched
back again to the shivering cul-
prit on the front stairs.

Children often exhibit a brilliancy of conception in the attainment
of their ends in view, which would bring no discredit on operations
of more importance, and by more experienced brains. The Auton
girls were forbidden to play with water because it wetted their
aprons and sleeves, and was spilt all over the nursery floor; and
above all it gave them sore throat. This was one of Mother Auton's inexorable commands. The question with the girls was how
to get round the command without disobeying the law.

Up in the "baby-house," and among the dolls, "washing-day" came about as regularly as it did down below in the laundry. The girls said the dolls' "duds" needed to go in the tub and be ironed every week, or else "their children would look like a family of emigrants."

Now A. Auton was a motherly girl, and "took" naturally to babies and their habits, and knew just the best way of "playing paper-dolls." It seemed to her indispensable that her children's dresses should be washed, yet how could she do it without water? So the little girl sat down and thought and thought, and after long

deliberation she concluded that she would "chew-out" the weekly wash, piece by piece. In that way her mother would not be disobeyed, yet her doll-children would be kept decent. So every Monday morning while Rosannah was washing in the laundry she sat up at the baby-house window and chewed and chewed her little dresses until her tiny jaws grew weary, and her salivary glands refused to perform their office. One dotted muslin tried her powers the most. It took more time and more chew to make that gown tidy than all the rest of the wash. I believe if she had swallowed what her little teeth ground out of that dotted muslin it would have killed her, but an open window into the yard provided a means of escape from this danger. Dear little mother !

CHAPTER TENTH.

AUTON KITCHEN.

T the risk of making a trite remark I will observe that the advent of spring gives me delightful emotions. The swelling buds cause a corresponding expansion of heart. The first sight of a robin tilting his tail and gushing forth his flute note, stirs within me an ecstasy. It is a delicious moment to the school-boy when he can throw off his overcoat and "comforter," for the days of sore throat, and salt and vinegar gargle, are numbered. Animals feel just like human beings at this vernal period. The cows chew their cud on the sunny side of the barn with a smile on their faces, and draw in great draughts of the balmy south wind with half-shut eyes. The hens and roosters pick up the Easter-worms and cock their heads about as if they pitied common mortals, who couldn't scratch up the warm, responsive earth. The doves come forth from their round holes and strut about in the sunshine, while the sleek kittens commence to charm the bluebirds, out of pure malice. Every opening year I renew my youth by this delicious experience. Men become boys again when they feel thus. The years that have rolled between youth and manhood are annihilated, and for the nonce we are, as we will be in eternity, with the notion of time entirely discounted and blotted out of our existence.

By the recurrence of these sensations, so common to every schoolboy, I return again to that youthful epoch when Rosannah the cook inhabited Auton kitchen. In bright bandanna and stern ebony countenance she stands before me, as I used to see her, arms akimbo, listening to the orders for the day.

Rosannah was cook in Auton House for nearly thirty years. She wore one little thin gold ring on the third finger of her well-formed, long, left hand, but we never knew whether she was ever married. I pity the rash youth who linked his fate to hers, because she who thoroughly believed in the old adage that "too many cooks spoil the broth" could surely dispense with any masculine suggestions in regard to the matrimonial pottage. It is safe to predict that if Rosannah ever was  a bride it must have been for a brief and sanguinary period. She was what might be termed a cross cook, but ah! was n't she a good one though? To watch her manipulate a Rhode Island turkey "going round doing good" in the bright tin-kitchen, gave one an appetite for dinner. Once on the skewer and before the roaring wood fire, it was a mere question of time that separated you from a dish fit for the gods. With the air of an expert she opened the roaster to inspect the savory process. Her dredger in one hand, and long spoon in the other, she "basted" the blistering bird with the flour, and poured the sputtering gravy over its magnificent breast, with all the dignity of a queen. When the turkey was ready to be served a fragrant cloud enveloped it which penetrated to the dining-room. The great mountain of breast was blistered and browned with half an inch of aromatic dressing. No tough, yellow pin-feathered legs stuck up before you, but lovely, bulging drum-sticks, dripping with gravy, and folded together in peaceful satis-faction. Its liver and manly gizzard were huddled together, just under the sides of the home where they lived, and a suspicion of onion and sweet marjoram permeated the air in the immediate vi-cinity.

Those ideal roast-turkey days took their flight when the new-fashioned bakers, and ranges, and cooking stoves, stuck their ugly faces into the kitchen. Anthracite coal can never charm forth the subtle qualities and evanescent flavors which lurk within the " sa-cred precincts " of this wonderful bird. It requires the magic heat of walnut and hickory to achieve this victory. An old-fashioned tin-kitchen, unstinted charcoal, a fresh fore-stick, with Rosannah the cook to superintend the operation, are the conditions which unlock the secret. What modern civilization is to the American Indian, so a new-fangled range was to our old cook. The two could not exist in company, so when the range entered at one door Rosannah and the yellow-eyed cat departed by the other. And with her fled the iron crane and the pot-hooks, the sooty horse-shoes and the Rumford's Roaster, the great brick oven and the old tin-kitchen, the biscuit baker and the Johnny-cake board. A new régime had dawned upon us, and baked turkey and tasteless meats usurped the places of juicy birds and "gissam" gravy.

We children had a great deal to do with Rosannah the cook. Like other children our appetites were perennial, and we flocked to her in troops for provender. She never would tell us what we were to have for dinner. The nearest she ever came to it was, "Lare overs for meddlers." Whether this expression was African for roast turkey or beefsteak we never knew. We stood about her like a swarm of bees, together with all the strange boys of the neighborhood who always came into the kitchen when there was anything to eat there. All hungry as bears, all famishing, all with remarkably good digestions. She looked down from her sable height upon the white brood beneath her. The ponderous loaf of brown bread rested in her left hand. With one scoop of the knife in her right she spread the whole surface with the yellow butter, with a single cut the slice was severed from the parent loaf and dealt out to the expectant boy, with another majestic look she repeated the operation until the crowd was filled.

"Now, g'long!" "Out with ye!" she cried, "Shut the doo'," and

6

the bread-and-butter brigade vanished from sight. Saturday night was a busy one in Rosannah's kitchen, because the Sunday morning's breakfast was being prepared. This meal, on that day, had been the same in Auton House for sixty years. Whatever may be said concerning the indigestibility of hot Indian pudding and baked beans, fish-balls, and brown bread, it is a fact that the Autons thrived on this diet.

But in order that these toothsome delicacies should become harmless, it was quite necessary that they be laid away in the hot brick oven during Saturday night to steam and simmer until the bells for Sunday-school commenced ringing in the morning.

The crackling flames of a dry wood fire licked and hugged the red sloping sides of the brick oven into a white heat. Rosannah stood ready to remove with tongs and hod the larger embers, and with the old turkey wing to spread an even layer of hot ashes over the brick bottom to prevent the precious viands from burning.

First, came the Indian pudding. This was set on the broad iron shovel and pushed to its position in the farthest corner of the oven. Then followed the brown bread which took its place on the right of its sweet relative, and last of all the beans. A delicate slice of choice pork just peeked over the rim of the dish as if to say, "*Au revoir mes amis,*" "*Au plaisir!*" Rosannah closed the oven with the great iron door. Her part of the work was over. The remainder of it was to be performed by the mysterious action of those subtle forces within the fiery chamber.

I must say a word about Rosannah's coffee. I know that the German beverage is very palatable, unter den linden; the French variety is delicious after dinner at **Trois frères**; the Egyptian compound requires the aid of narghili and tarbooshe to make it tolerable, while the English liquid is not to be mentioned. All these are good in their way, but Rosannah's coffee was perfect nectar. She burnt it, and ground it, and boiled it herself, and then she settled it with a fish-skin and egg-shells in the tall tin coffee-pot.

The fragrance of that "Old Government Java," while it was being parched, came 'way out into the front entry. Rosannah stirred the berries with one particular burnt stick, which gave it a certain mysterious flavor. She always parched the coffee Saturday afternoons, at the gloaming, and before the lamps were lighted.

Vi'lette Jackson usually sat by the fireside, smoking her short pipe, and watching the operation. Those two weird, ebony women, in bright bandannas and solemn mien, looked like witches as they stirred round the fragrant compound by the flickering fire-light.

The big coffee-pot was allowed to stand a while on the warm hearth to insure greater purity to its contents, then Rosannah held the bright vessel aloft, one elbow on hip, and poured the dark aromatic tide by graceful curves into the vasty depths of the family urn. The heater was next plunged into the bubbling caldron, and Jenny carried it to the dining-room.

Rosannah seldom smiled.

Rosannah seldom talked.

Her business was to cook, and she attended to her business. On washing days she had a half tumbler of spirits to keep off "rheumatiz." She wore a wadded hood and "india-rubbers" when she hung out the clothes on Mondays. She was very superstitious, and believed that the horse-shoes she had hung on the old crane kept off the witches. To see Rosannah out of the kitchen and in her best bonnet, you would never recognize her. On the public streets her countenance wore a sad and depressed expression. She was out of her element there; but once in her kitchen, with a fresh bandanna about her head, and she was "monarch of all she surveyed."

Her wadded-hood.

Her India Rubbers.

Her last tumbler of gin and...

Father Auton being quite epicurean in his taste. Rosannah the cook and he were naturally *en rapport*. For she knew just how long to cook his venison, and just the extra pinch of spice to put in his calf's-head soup, and just the amount of brandy for his mince pies. Her roast pig on Fourth of Julys would have delighted Charles Lamb, and her potted-pigeon gravy was the wonder of the neighborhood. When she was complimented on her success she rewarded her friends by the grim apparition of a smile, which soon blended again into her ordinary stoicism.

It is poor policy to moralize about cooks, but I must indulge in it for a moment now. There would have been no Auton kitchen to speak about if there had been no Rosannah to go into it, and without a kitchen Auton House could not have existed for a day, and had there been no Auton House there would have been no Auton family, so it seems clear that the whole autonomy of the Autons depended upon the life of one good, cross old black woman.

I pity cooks. Their wages would be cheap, it seems to me, were they five times what they are. With an old-fashioned cook in a family, the father and mother agree, the children are always healthy and hungry, and one entertains his friends with no jar or excitement. Without such an one everybody is "at sea" at once, and the whole family degenerates into a lot of quarreling tramps. A good cook is a boon in disguise, even a bad one is better than none.

In those Rosannah days, your cook, your minister, and your home were known quantities; nowadays they are all just the other way. Then, people were content to remain at home during the hottest weather, behind the closed blinds and in cool retreat, within their comfortable chambers; now they are frantic to sit on their trunks killing mosquitoes, in a closet at the top of a wooden caravansary, at ten dollars per day, and say they are happy. People used to go to the "Springs," in August, to drink the waters, and lived contentedly at home the rest of the year. Nowadays, on the contrary, they do quite the reverse.

Auton kitchen ran on without stopping for fifty years. Good, faithful Rosannah! She has cooked her last turkey, she has made her last pie, and the secret of her seasoning departed with her. With slight paraphrase, the dying words attributed to that "tired old woman" would be applicable to her: —

> "Her last words on earth were: 'Dear friends, I am going
> Where washing ain't done, nor starching nor sewing,
> And everything there will be just to my wishes,
> For where they don't eat there 's no washing of dishes.
> I'll be where loud anthems will always be ringing,
> But having no voice I'll get rid of the singing.
> Don't mourn for me now, don't mourn for me never,
> For I'm going to do nothing for ever and ever.'"

CHAPTER ELEVENTH.

CHRISTMAS AT AUTON HOUSE.

QUEER as it may seem, the Autons never hung up their stockings at Christmas. They put out their shoes instead. Why it was so is a question, but as no Auton ever did it, no Auton ever would. We regularly sang, however, Mr. Moore's "Night before Christmas," and thought we had fully complied with the requirements of the lines: —

> "The stockings were hung by the chimney with care,
> In the hopes that St. Nicholas soon would be there."

Possibly this departure from the ancient rule arose from our custom of receiving presents after breakfast, and also that our great, great, great grandmother was a French Huguenot, and preferred the sabot. We only troubled Santa Claus in the early morning for a bundle of candy, and such other knickknacks as he might feel inclined to bestow.

Our boots and shoes being the chosen vessels to receive this early freight, they were set on the mahogany table in the upper hall, and were ranged from father's down to the eleventh Auton's in regular gradation.

Our big brother was expected home by the early boat, so *that*, together with other anticipations, drove sleep from our pillows. From hour to hour on the night preceding Christmas we raised

our uneasy, tumbled heads from our couches, hoping it was light enough to scream out, in one word, " wishy'rmerryChristmas," but somehow the sun stuck down and would n't " hurry up." But at the faintest suspicion of dawn we thumped poor Deb'rah with our feet to go for our shoes. Oh! how dead with sleep that much-abused nurse used to be, curled up on the edge of the bed! Knowing that she would be called upon at a moment's notice, this model guardian of babyhood always kept about her a flannel garment, ready to fly at the first thump. I can remember, as if it were yesterday, just how that flannel petticoat felt to my boyish feet as I pushed and pushed her, little by little, off the edge of the bed to wake her up.

As the sun mounted the heavens six or eight Autons, with shoes before them, sat bolt upright in bed destroying their appetites.

By eight o'clock Auton nursery was nauseated, and the bare idea of breakfast was revolting. Our big brother, however, was not at all excited by this exceptional state of things. He drank his coffee, ate his " drop cakes " and conversed with Father Auton about the news from the metropolis as if there never was any such thing as Christmas. With one leg crossed contentedly over the other he read, and read, and read the morning paper until we children were fairly exasperated with him. There could be no fun upstairs until he came, because Mother Auton would have waited for him a whole day, if necessary, before distributing the presents.

To our great relief he joined at last the noisy throng as it swept like a breeze up the front stairs into "mother's room."

Deb'rah's small-armed half-sister "Ruby" used to say, when inquiry was made concerning her health, "that she was pretty poorly," and that expresses the state of Mother Auton's feelings a good deal of the time at that epoch. She thought that each Christmas would be the last one she was to be with us, so that in the midst of our hilarity we always had a tear in one eye. If the amount of delight which danced in our expectant hearts on those Christmas mornings could have been fairly put into the scales and held there long enough they would have weighed down a continent.

Mother Auton went to one particular deep drawer, in one particular bureau, on one particular side of the room, and there, standing before its open mouth, with tears in her dear eyes and a trembling in her speech, she placed in our hands the little tokens of her affection, one after another, from father down to Rosannah the cook, with such little speeches as : —

" Accept this, my dear, as a fond token of affection from your mother," etc.; and " This silk, dear E., was the nearest I could get like the one you wanted so much," etc.; or " Take this remembrance. C. Auton, from your loving mother," etc.; and " This, my darling, is a small affair, but," etc., etc., etc. And so she went down the whole row, keeping us just between smiles and tears all the time, until the festival was closed. Dear, dear Mother Auton !

The remembrance of those beatific days, that mystic association which clings to Christmas-tide, and the precious memories which they bring to us of maternal love and noble unselfishness, have imparted strength to endure that bitter burden of disappointment and death which sooner or later falls to the lot of every human creature.

CHAPTER TWELFTH.

FATHER AUTON.

THAT boy is fortunate who has reason to be proud of his father. We Auton boys were lucky fellows in this respect. When people told us that they knew we were " Autons " by our resemblance to " our daddy," we were ready to hug them with delight. At school we stood prepared to fight at a moment's notice to see whose father was the strongest. We had many youthful arguments to sustain our lofty estimate of his character ; for, said we, " did n't he manage a bank which was broken into ?" and " was n't he in the city government and a visitor to the insane asylum ?" and " did n't he speak to all the poor people in town, and say 'sarvant, marm,' to the women, and 'savant, sir,' to the men ?" and " did n't he carry a gold-headed cane which he thumped along the sidewalks ?" and " did n't the butcher hang up venison all winter for him, and then bring in great long bills in the spring, which he had to turn over and over and over again before he got to the end of them ?" and " did n't he indorse pretty promissory notes for Cousin Ezra, and then pay up all Cousin Ezra's pretty debts for him ?" and " did n't he have what Mother Auton called ' a corporation.' Now," reasoned we, "how could he do all these wonderful things and have all these wonderful traits unless he was a wonderful man?" The fact was self-evident.

I remember so well that delicate suspicion of tobacco which lingered about his hands, and which we used to sniff whenever he played with us: "Barber! barber! shaved a mason," or boxed our ears in earnest; on these latter occasions his great hands weighed a ton, and for that reason we begged Mother Auton to do all the family castigation — it was so short and soon over.

In those days Father Auton went to market early every morning with his basket on his arm, often accompanied by some of his "boys." He sauntered about from cart to cart inspecting the fresh and tempting merchandise in the cool morning air.

It was quite a blow to youthful pride, sometimes, to be sent home from the butcher's wagon with a big cock-turkey dangling between one's legs, and its gorgeous tail spreading its ample plumage before one like a fan. Father Auton chuckled to himself when he practiced this little joke upon his "rising" sons. It is proper, however, to remark that this duty was never shirked, but with cane and kids in one hand, and cock-turkey in the other, the "rising son,"

bowing and scraping to the friends who met him, triumphantly carried the dangling monster safely through the main streets, and laid
his yellow carcase in Auton kitchen. In those days all the black-
berries and huckle-berries were peddled from house to house. Father Auton used to go out to the farmer's wagon without his hat,
and inspect the coal-black fruit which lay before him in half-bushel
measures instead of scanty quart boxes of the present day. In those

times it was expected that people would " try " the berries before
purchasing them. The way was to scoop up a little heap in the
palm of one's hand, and shake them up a bit to get them well together: then pour them down the throat like peas in a hopper.
Father Auton generally ended these " trials " by taking five or six
quarts.

Auton kitchen consumed charcoal by the load. Great deep baskets of it were sold at six and eight cents, and the tally used to be kept on the back of the wood-house door; one, two, three, four, and then a mark across like this: until the hundred and fifty baskets were deposited in the bins. Farmers brought in from the country towering loads of walnut and hickory, which they pitched over into the cobble-stoned yard of Auton House, while the oxen and the old horse munched corn-stalks and hay in the lane.

Every family had its own wood-sawyer in those days. We had ours, named " Daddy Burns." This individual was as tall as a sycamore, and as red as a peony. He had a bald head, and a red flannel cap, which he put on when he " sawed." He wore a short jacket and a little flat black hat. His e n o r m o u s trousers had nothing to mark them but patches and amplitude, while his thick cow-hide shoes seemed to inclose a

pair of " hoofs " instead of feet. He must have been six feet and a half in height. He came swaying into Auton yard like the mainmast of a ship, with his saw in one hand and his horse in the other, looking like a son of Anak. Daddy Burns had a grand old face, a mixture of the patriarch and the inebriate. He never laughed, but lived a lonely and dignified existence far above the heads of other men.

He was seldom in good spirits, but very frequently in bad ones. He really loved rum for rum's sake, and his long throat made him an excellent judge of it. He or some other family wood-sawyer was the one who drank two large bowls of chocolate without stopping, and then said he "did n't like choc'late."

Father Auton used to lay in the potatoes, and the turnips and carrots, by the hundred bushels every winter. I seem to hear now the echo of their tumbling into the big bins down cellar, as basket after basket deposited its rumbling contents. "Nick Peters," "Old Speywood," and "Mr. Atwood" brought to Father Auton his "Carolina-potatoes," his "soft-soap," and his "freckled pippin-apples." Old Speywood was an Indian, Nick Peters was a "Portugee," and Mr. Atwood was a Yankee, — all very unique varieties of men. Peters was short and the color of a cent; Speywood had straight black hair and high cheek bones, and when he plunged his dipper into the soft-soap barrel he seemed to be on the point of giving his native "war-whoop," and leaping from his wagon to "scalp" some of us; while Mr. Atwood had a perennial smile on his face not unlike his pippins, and often stopped in his work to give us a golden specimen out of the barrels in his cart. These men were great friends with Father Auton, and well they might be, for they supplied the needs of Auton House for many years at good prices. Our butter and milk were kept fresh and cool down the well, in a tidy, unpainted wooden box, which preserved these articles quite as perfectly as the modern refrigerator.

The style of living in those days was simpler than the present régime, and had a corresponding influence upon the habits and customs of society. Men and women lived long and slept better than they do nowadays; but it must be acknowledged that Father Auton was what "our Deb'rah" called a "snorer." The "long-drawn notes of his bugle," as they rose and fell on the silent summer air, used to startle us from our slumber during those sweltering August nights when all the windows were open. In depth and compass they surpassed the chronic concert of tree-toad and festive bull-frog.

His youthful feelings, his sympathizing nature, and his love of humor made Father Auton the very best of companions. It was a treat to see him make a quill-pen. After scraping the proper portion with the back of his knife-blade, he laid the nib on the nail of his left thumb, and performed the operation with the air of a professor. Nobody knew better than he did a chicken from a fowl, and he told a story almost as well as "Uncle Josiah." In summer he suffered fearfully from the heat, and used to plunge his whole head in the great brass basin filled with sparkling pump-water, like a Newfoundland dog, and lay his hot hands, as far as the elbows, in the same refreshing element when he returned from the "office." His teeth were like ivory; and his favorite way of amusing the youngsters of the family was to seize them by wrist and opposite leg, swing them back and forth through the air, and then blow in their faces.

Father Auton was our first teacher both in drawing and penmanship. He showed us how to make an eagle by the flourish of a pen. He set our first "copy" in the writing book: "Let beauty shine in every line," and puzzled us by saying that p-o-t spelt tea-pot, and l-o-o-t spelt elder-blow tea.

Unfortunate is the boy who loses his father before he becomes a
man. A symmetrical character needs the influence of both the
male and female natures during the critical period of youth. Neither the maternal nor the paternal influence alone can form a perfect character. A boy brought up entirely by the mother becomes
a man from a woman's point of view, and is apt to be wanting in
those qualities most needed in the battle with the world; while a
youth who attains maturity unaided by the subtle potency of maternal influence is likely to possess a harsh and one-sided disposition,
and too often becomes tyrannical and brutal. It requires two sensi-
ble persons, a man and a woman, to round out and perfect the
manly character. Some wiseacre has remarked that " It is easy
enough to get another wife, but where on earth can you get another mother?" This axiom can be matched by what old Aunt
Katy (the black ironer of Auton kitchen) said one day, when the
conversation turned upon the merits of Father Auton : —

"'Tain't no use talkin'; I would n't giv' nuffin' for these 'ere
step-faders! Callin' a man 'fader' don't make him fader, does n't
it? Brack or white, a chile wid'out a fresh and bloody fader ain't
got no show 't all, honey!"

"A boy is father to the man." His character resembles a kernel of corn possessing great possibilities, which depend upon the accidents of soil, sunshine, and rain, to develop into a harvest. There is something subtle and intangible in a boy's nature, which makes him walk and talk like his father when he grows up, no matter if he be nurtured on the plains of Arabia, or fed on missionaries in the South Sea islands. We are the same creatures in old age that we are in youth, plus a few cares and anxieties, losses and disappointments which have been put upon us in the journey of life, weighing us down like heavy garments. Although it is true that to eat of the tree of knowledge is to cease being a brute and commence being an angel, still it is the acquirement of that same knowledge which causes our bitterest tears to flow, and furrows up our brows with care.

A little extra knowledge which we gained at ten years is what

7

killed "Santa Claus" forever, and stopped up one avenue of the
keenest joy. It is nothing but increased intelligence which prevents
us in our manhood from indulging with zest in the sports of our
youth. For instance, nowadays, after we have gone through the
operation of "winding up" and "pegging down" our top in the
ring, say eight times running, our improved minds tell us that we
have "extracted all the juice out of that lemon," and there is
nothing more to express, thereby spoiling all our fun in that direc-
tion forever. How true it is that "where ignorance is bliss 't is folly
to be wise." Boyhood is the age of anticipation, which, again,
knowledge and experience ruin and dissipate forever. Take, for
example, the ecstasy of lying awake on Friday nights "contem-
plating the coming" joys of Saturday. There is no pleasure equal
to it. The real bliss of our holiday, when it actually arrived, did
not compare with the ideal presentment of it; indeed, it was no
pleasure at all if it had happened to be a rainy day, and this pleasure consisted in our want of knowledge of the true facts of the
case. Youthful disappointments, too, are easily "discounted," and
in that unsuspecting era, having no knowledge, we recovered from
them as easily as we did when we "bark'd our shins."

There are many occasions in maturity when a man's feelings are
identical with those of his boyhood. I remember how I disliked
strangers and fled from their society, how I hated to be questioned,
and shrank from exerting myself where I was unacquainted, and
how unpleasant it used to be when called from the play-ground into
the drawing-room of Auton House, to be asked my name, and if I
could "spell cat," etc. I smile to myself nowadays when I think
how little I am changed from that early period. For instance, when
I enter a modern ball-room and see before me the spacious apart-

ments redolent with the fragrance of flowers, the air palpitating with inspiring music. polychrome-women and neatly attired men parading through the lighted vistas. the buzz of conversation filling the ear, and the potent charm which refinement imparts. putting a spell upon me, I don't know whether to go in and sit down. or go out and stand up. I am impatient if I am talking with one person to leave him and go and talk to another. I desire to flee away. I feel a mad impulse to break from my dearest friend and rush up-stairs, down-stairs, anywhere but remain quiet where I am. It is the identical feeling that used to possess me on those nights when Deb'rah dressed me up in my new "Aunt-Nancy-Miller suit," for one of Mother Anton's parties, and with wild eyes (like the "wandering Jew" impelled along by the invisible command, "Marchez!" "marchez!") I flew from the top of the house to the kitchen until the party was over. and the smoke from the sputtering candles filled the darkened apartments. Could we only throw off our experiences, one by one, as we do our garments. we should at last become like little children again. The successive layers of care and trouble, which fall to the lot of everybody. obliterate the boyish character and bury the youthful heart beneath their gravity and ugliness. We only realize that, underneath it all, there still exists, 'way down below, a perennial fount of youth. which old age cannot quench. nor disease quite dry up, and which it is possible to hear whenever we pause long enough on the dusty thoroughfare of life to listen to the merry murmur of its waters.